Are We Nearly There Yet?

Read more books in this series:

Apples Are Magic!	My First Day
I Want That!	Tell Us a Bedtime Story
It's My Party!	The Noisy Night Monsters
My Family's Fantastic!	Where Are You, Mr Moo?

Will You Be My Friend?

www.sainsburysentertainment.co.uk

ARE WE NEARLY THERE YET?
A PICTURE CORGI BOOK 978 0 552 56814 2
Published in Great Britain exclusively for Sainsbury's
by Picture Corgi, an imprint of Random House Children's Publishers UK
A Random House Group Company
This edition published 2013

1 3 5 7 9 10 8 6 4 2

Copyright © Random House Children's Publishers UK, 2013
Illustrated by Julia Seal
The right of Julia Seal to be identified as the illustrator of this work has
been asserted in accordance with the Copyright, Designs and Patents Act 1988.

Picture Corgi Books are published by Random House Children's Publishers UK,
61–63 Uxbridge Road, London W5 5SA
www.randomhousechildrens.co.uk
www.randomhouse.co.uk
Addresses for companies within The Random House Group Limited can be found at:
www.randomhouse.co.uk/offices.htm
THE RANDOM HOUSE GROUP Limited Reg. No. 954009
A CIP catalogue record for this book is available from the British Library.
Printed in China

MIX
Paper from
responsible sources
FSC® C020056

The Random House Group Limited supports the Forest Stewardship Council (FSC®), the leading international
forest certification organization. Our books carrying the FSC label are printed on FSC®-certified paper.
FSC is the only forest certification scheme endorsed by the leading environmental organizations, including
Greenpeace. Our paper procurement policy can be found at www.randomhouse.co.uk/environment.

Are We Nearly There Yet?

Illustrated by Julia Seal

Picture Corgi

Ruby and Theo were setting off with Mum and Dad to visit Granny in the country.

They made sure they had everything they might need.

First they waited for the bus at the bus stop.
But when it finally arrived . . .

. . . the bus went very, very slowly.
"Are we nearly there yet?" asked Ruby and Theo.
"Not yet," said Mum.

"I know why it's so slow," whispered Theo.

"A wicked witch has cast a spell on the bus!"

"We'll need to wait for a good wizard to stop her!"
said Ruby.

Eventually they arrived at the station, just as the train was getting ready to set off.

But the train kept stopping for no reason.
"Are we nearly there yet?" asked Ruby and Theo.
"Not yet," said Dad.

"I know why it keeps stopping," whispered Ruby.

"All the animals must have escaped from the zoo and got on to the track!"

"We'll have to wait for the police and the fire brigade to catch them and take them home," said Theo.

Finally they reached Granny's station, where they took a taxi. The taxi driver was very friendly and asked all about their journey.

But the taxi got stuck in a huge traffic jam.
"Are we nearly there yet?" asked Ruby and Theo.
"Not yet," said Mum and Dad together.
"We'll be there soon."

"I know why there's a traffic jam," whispered Theo.

"There's treasure buried in the road up ahead and pirates are digging it up!"

"We'll have to wait for the dragon who guards the treasure to scare them away," said Ruby.

At last the taxi got moving.
"Are we nearly there yet?" Dad asked Mum
with a grin.

"It does feel like the longest journey ever," Mum laughed.

"I think Granny's house must have sprouted legs and be running away from us," said Dad.

"Yes, we're going to need a giant to catch it for us!" shouted Ruby and Theo together.

Finally the taxi reached Granny's house.
And there was Granny waiting.
"You poor things," said Granny. "You must have
had a terrible journey."

"No, it was the best journey ever!" said Ruby and Theo. "There was a witch, and an elephant and pirates and a dragon …"

"Goodness! It does sound like an exciting journey!" said Granny, helping them into the house.

"Well, you'll just have to come and visit more often," she smiled, giving Ruby and Theo a big hug.